In memory of my mother who was always there for me,
which was priceless ~ T.C.

For baby O and Mom ~ T.N.

tiger tales
5 River Road, Suite 128, Wilton, CT 06897
Published in the United States 2019
Originally published in Great Britain 2019
by Little Tiger Press Ltd.
Text copyright © 2019 Tracey Corderoy
Illustrations copyright © 2019 Tony Neal
ISBN-13: 978-1-68010-175-1
ISBN-10: 1-68010-175-7
Printed in China
LTP/1400/2653/0219

For more insight and activities,
visit us at www.tigertalesbooks.com

SNEAKY BEAK

by Tracey Corderoy

Illustrated by Tony Neal

tiger tales

Bear and Hamster were enjoying their favorite television show when suddenly it stopped for a **commercial**. "Not that **Sneaky Beak** again!" muttered Bear. "What is it this time . . . ?"

IS YOUR BED
BOUNCY ENOUGH?
Our *Snores-Galore Mega Bed* is the bounciest EVER. Sweet dreams guaranteed every night!
Call for a bounce test on your old bed
NOW!
CALL NOW!!
SB

"A bounce test!" chuckled Bear.

"Oh, Hamster, what next?!"

But late that night, Bear started to think . . . .

Was that a broken spring?

And was his mattress sagging?

As Hamster snored, Bear just couldn't sleep.
"Oh, no!" he cried. "What if my bed
ISN'T bouncy enough after all?!"
And he tossed and turned all night long.

First thing in the morning, Bear called for a bounce test,
and Sneaky Beak **zoomed** up in a van.

Hello! Trouble sleeping?
That simply won't do!
If you need a new bed,
Here's a deal just for you!

His bounce test bunnies got right to work.

Then Sneaky Beak checked the report.
"Thank goodness you called, Bear!" he said with a gasp.
"This bed is **completely** out of bounce. You need the
Snores-Galore Mega Bed right away!"

But Bear's new bouncy bed was **enormous**.
There wasn't room for anything else.
"Wait!" Bear cried as Hamster's things were carted out.
"Sweet dreams!" replied Sneaky Beak. "Oh! But remember:
you'll sleep better after a nice **bubble bath**."
He handed Bear a flyer and was gone.

"A WHAT??!" gulped Bear,
and he started to read . . .

IS YOUR BATH BUBBLY ENOUGH?

Our Super-Whirl
Turbo Tub has it ALL!

Wave machine, bubble-blowers,
jets — and more!

Call **NOW!**

Bear shook his head. "Our old
tub is just fine!" But at bathtime . . .

. . . he wasn't so sure!

"Gosh! What if our bath ISN'T bubbly enough?!" he cried. Uh-oh . . . .

Bear called Sneaky Beak at once, who rumbled up in a 10-ton truck.

Hello! Tiny bubbles?
That simply won't do!
If you need a new tub,
Here's a deal just for you!

It came with boxfuls of knobs and hoses
that soon filled the entire bathroom.
"Marvelous choice!"
Sneaky Beak chirped when
at last the job was done.

TURBO

"Ooo! What does this twirly thing do?"
wondered Bear.
And they soon found out . . . .

The next morning at breakfast, Bear was waiting with a present.
"Here, Hamster! To cheer you up," he said.

"It's a *Crunch-O-Matic Granola Maker*, see?"

"The thing is," he explained, "I was starting to worry that our cereal wasn't **CRUNCHY** enough!
Don't start the day with a soggy snack—bring that crunchy goodness back!"

Crunch
-O-
Matic

oats

NUTS

He plugged it in, and Hamster waited as the oats and raisins softly swirled.
Then with a clunk and a whirr . . .

Hamster's present hadn't cheered him up **AT ALL**.
"We need a vacation,"
Bear said with a sigh.

Then two beady eyes peeked in . . . .

Hello!
Feeling glum?
Need a break from
this place . . . ?

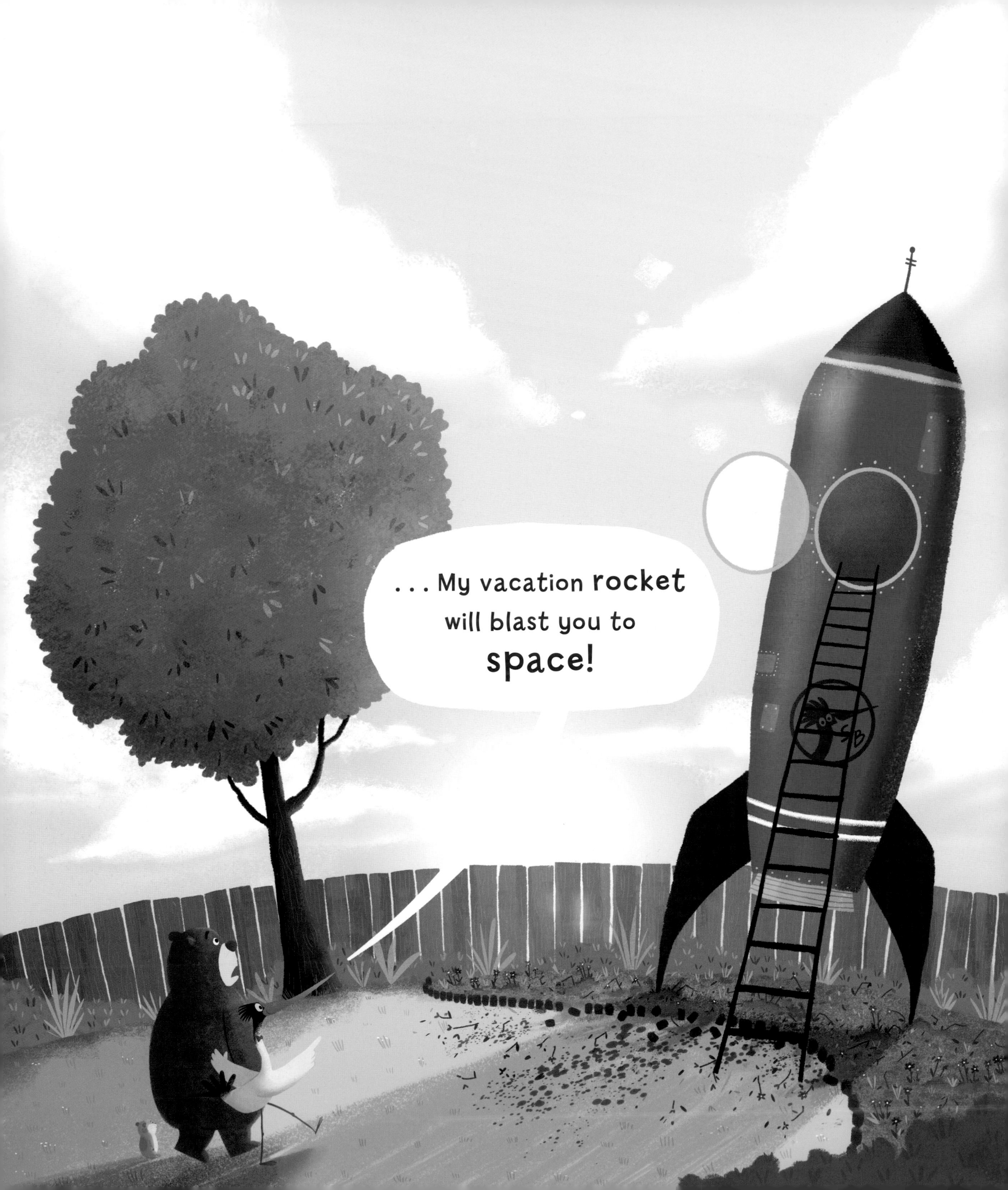
. . . My vacation rocket will blast you to space!

In a blink, Bear was whisked up into the rocket.
Then — *ZOOM* — he was soaring through the sky,
while Hamster was getting farther and farther away.

Outer space was really quiet and calm.
It was the perfect place to think.
"How silly I've been," whispered Bear,
"changing beds, and bathtubs, and breakfasts."
What made him happiest of all was
none of those things.

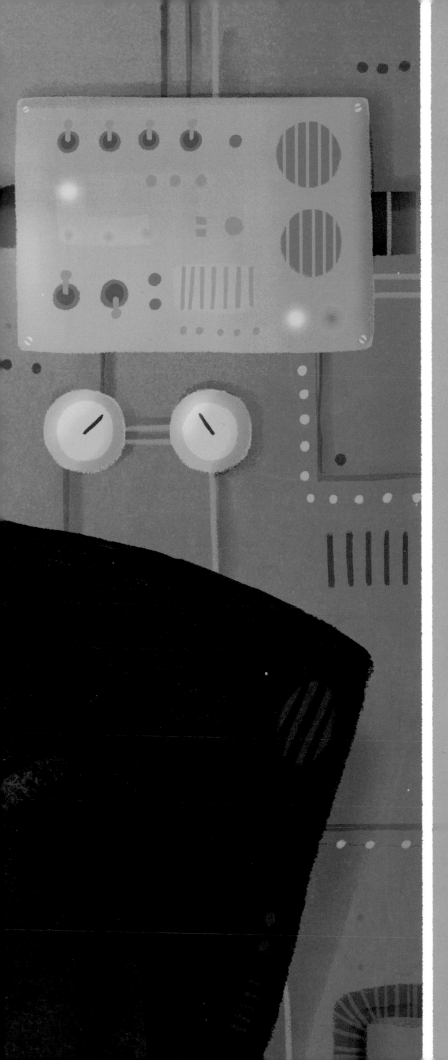

So Bear set the rocket's dial
to take him right back home . . .

SPACE   HOME

. . . to the friend he wouldn't change for anything.

"Oh, Hamster!" said Bear.

"I've missed you!"

Bear and Hamster cleaned up together.
Their new stuff was just getting in the way.

"The question," said Bear, "is what are we going to **do** with it all?"

With that, a beak poked in through the mail slot.

IS YOUR GARBAGE CAN BIG ENOUGH?
Our new *Trash-tastic Trash Cans* will hold **ALL** your unwanted garbage!

Open your door to test one out **NOW!**

Bear folded his arms.
"No, thanks!" he called back . . .

"...Hamster and I will **recycle!**"

From then on, things were simply fine.
Bear and Hamster had each other,
and that was all they needed.

But Sneaky Beak's trash can did come in rather handy after all!